MC

Nighttime secrets and dreams in a romance to remember

Sandra Sandoval

TABLE OF CONTENTS

Chapter 1: Moonlit Whispers 4
    The First Encounter 4
    A Dance Beneath the Stars 6
    Secrets Shared in the Night 9

Chapter 2: Dreams and Desires 13
    Unveiling Hidden Longings 13
    Whispers of the Heart 16
    Midnight Confessions 18

Chapter 3: Shadows of the Past 22
    Echoes of Forgotten Love 22
    Unraveling Old Wounds 25
    Choices and Consequences 27

Chapter 4: Starlit Promises 31
    A Pledge Under the Moon 31
    Holding Onto Hope 33
    The Weight of a Promise 36

Chapter 5: The Dance of Fate 40
    Serendipitous Meetings 40
    The Pull of Destiny 43
    Crossroads of the Heart 45

Chapter 6: Twilight Revelations 49
    Truths in the Night 49

  The Unspoken Bond 52
  Unveiling the Mask 55

Chapter 7: Love's Labyrinth 58
  Navigating the Maze 58
  Torn Between Two Worlds 60
  The Journey Within 63

Chapter 8: The Light of Love 67
  A Beacon in the Darkness 67
  Embracing the Dawn 69
  A Love Reborn 72

Chapter 9: Moonlight and Memories 76
  A Night to Remember 76
  The Threads of Time 78
  An Everlasting Embrace 81

Chapter 10: A New Dawn 85
  The Promise of Tomorrow 85
  Building a Future Together 87
  The Eternal Dance 90

CHAPTER 1: MOONLIT WHISPERS

The First Encounter

Under the gentle glow of the moon, the world felt different—softer, more mysterious, and full of possibilities. The night air was crisp and carried a faint scent of blooming jasmine, adding an intoxicating allure to the evening. It was on such a night that Emma found herself wandering through the deserted gardens of the estate, her steps guided by nothing more than an unexplained yearning.

Emma had attended the charity gala out of obligation, her heart not quite in it. The event was a swirl of elegant gowns and polite conversation, but she felt detached, a spectator in her own life. As she drifted away from the crowd, the soft strains of music faded, leaving her with the comforting solitude of the night.

Her thoughts were interrupted when she noticed a figure silhouetted against the moonlit path. He stood with a quiet confidence, his gaze fixed on the sky as if seeking answers from the stars. Intrigued, Emma hesitated, unsure whether to approach or retreat. But the pull was undeniable, as if fate had orchestrated this moment just for them.

"Beautiful, isn't it?" His voice was deep, smooth, resonating with a warmth that seemed to melt the distance between them. Emma found herself drawn to the stranger, his presence both calming and electric.

"It is," she replied softly, stepping closer. Her curiosity piqued, she studied his features in the silvery light. His eyes, a deep shade of blue, reflected the moon's glow, and there was a certain kind of magic in the way he looked at her, as if seeing beyond the surface.

"I'm Alex," he introduced himself, offering a hand. His touch was gentle yet firm, grounding her in the moment.

"Emma," she replied, a smile playing on her lips. There was something about him that felt familiar, as if they were two souls who had shared countless lifetimes.

They talked about everything and nothing, their conversation flowing as naturally as the breeze that rustled the leaves. It was easy to lose track of time, the night wrapping around them like a comforting cloak. Emma found herself sharing stories she rarely told, drawn by an inexplicable trust in this stranger who felt like a kindred spirit.

As they wandered deeper into the gardens, the moonlight casting playful shadows, Emma felt a shift within her—a quiet awakening of emotions she had long kept at bay. There was something liberating about being seen, truly seen, by someone who was a perfect stranger yet felt like a missing piece.

When it was time to return to the real world, a part of her hesitated. But Alex, with a gentle smile, promised they'd meet again. "The night has a way of bringing people together," he said, his words a promise that lingered in the air.

Emma watched as he disappeared into the shadows, her heart lighter than it had been in years. The encounter had been brief, but it left an indelible mark—a whisper of something more, something magical, illuminated by the moon's gentle glow.

A Dance Beneath the Stars

The gala's main ballroom was a spectacle of opulence, with crystal chandeliers casting a warm glow over the assembled guests. Yet, for Emma, the true allure lay outside, where the night sky stretched endlessly above, dotted with countless stars. The evening air was refreshing, a gentle reminder of the world beyond the confines of the ballroom.

As Emma stepped out onto the terrace, she found herself once again drawn to the gardens. The soft strains of a waltz drifted through the air, a hauntingly beautiful melody that seemed to call her name. Her heart quickened with anticipation, her thoughts returning to Alex and their first encounter under the moonlit sky.

It was as if the universe had conspired to bring them together once more. Alex stood at the edge of the garden, his silhouette a familiar and comforting sight. He turned as she approached, his eyes lighting up with a warmth that mirrored her own.

"Emma," he greeted her, his voice a gentle caress in the night. "I hoped you'd come."

She smiled, a sense of rightness settling over her. "I couldn't resist." There was a shared understanding between them, an unspoken agreement that their connection was something special.

The music from the ballroom shifted to a lively tune, and Alex extended a hand, his eyes twinkling with mischief. "May I have this dance?"

Emma hesitated for only a moment before placing her hand in his. The world around them seemed to fade away as they moved in perfect harmony, their steps guided by the rhythm of the music and the silent song of the stars above.

Dancing with Alex felt like a revelation, each turn and sway a testament to the unspoken bond that had formed between them. The garden, bathed in the soft glow of moonlight, became their private ballroom, a sanctuary where time stood still.

Their laughter mingled with the music, a joyful sound that echoed in the night. Emma felt herself letting go, her heart opening to the possibilities that lay before her. She had spent so long guarding her emotions, but with Alex, it was different. He made her feel seen, cherished, and alive in a way she hadn't thought possible.

As the final notes of the waltz faded into the night, they found themselves standing close, their breaths mingling in the cool air. Emma looked up, meeting Alex's gaze, and knew that this was only the beginning of something extraordinary.

"Thank you," she whispered, her voice barely audible above the whisper of the wind.

"For what?" he asked, a teasing smile on his lips.

"For this," she replied, gesturing to the starlit garden around them. "For being here."

Alex chuckled softly, his eyes never leaving hers. "The night has a way of bringing people together, doesn't it?"

Emma nodded, her heart full of hope and promise. Beneath the stars, in the embrace of the night, she felt as if she had found a piece of herself she hadn't realized was missing.

As they stood there, wrapped in the magic of the moment, Emma knew that whatever the future held, she was ready to face it. With Alex by her side, anything was possible. The night, with all its secrets and dreams, was theirs to explore.

Secrets Shared in the Night

The garden, with its winding paths and fragrant blossoms, had become a familiar refuge for Emma and Alex. It was here, under the watchful gaze of the moon, that their connection deepened, unfurling like the petals of a night-blooming flower. The nights they spent together were filled with whispered conversations, each word revealing more of the person beneath the surface.

On one such night, the air was thick with anticipation, as if the stars themselves held their breath for what was to come. Emma and Alex walked side by side, their footsteps synchronized, each attuned to the other's presence.

The conversation flowed easily, a dance of words that mirrored their earlier waltz. They spoke of dreams and aspirations, of worlds they wished to explore and adventures yet to unfold. But as the hours slipped by, the topics turned more intimate, like shadows lengthening with the setting sun.

Emma paused, her gaze fixed on a cluster of night-blooming flowers, their scent heady and sweet. She took a deep breath, steadying herself, before turning to Alex. "There's something I need to tell you," she said, her voice tinged with vulnerability.

Alex stopped, his expression open and patient, a silent invitation for her to continue. "You can tell me anything, Emma."

His reassurance gave her the courage to share a piece of herself she had kept hidden for far too long. "I've always been afraid of letting people in," she confessed, her eyes searching his for understanding. "I've built walls to protect myself, but with you... it's different."

Alex nodded, his gaze unwavering. "I understand," he replied softly. "I've been there too."

Encouraged by his honesty, Emma pressed on. "Being here with you, it feels like I'm finally able to let those walls down. It's terrifying and exhilarating at the same time."

Alex reached for her hand, his touch grounding her. "We all have our secrets, Emma. But sharing them... it makes us stronger, don't you think?"

A comfortable silence settled between them, the night wrapping them in its embrace. It was a silence filled with promise, a testament to the trust they had built. Emma knew that whatever fears lingered, they could face them together.

As if sensing her thoughts, Alex spoke again, his voice a gentle murmur against the backdrop of the night. "There's something I've been meaning to tell you too."

Emma's heart skipped a beat, her curiosity piqued. She waited, sensing the weight of his words before he even spoke them.

"I've always been drawn to the night," Alex began, his eyes reflecting the moonlight. "It feels like a world apart, a place where anything is possible. But I never imagined I'd find someone who shares that same wonder."

His words struck a chord within her, a resonance that echoed deep in her soul. In that moment, Emma realized that their connection was not just a fleeting spark but a steady flame, nurtured by the secrets they shared and the dreams they dared to reveal.

As the night wore on, they continued to talk, each story a thread weaving them closer together. The garden bore witness to their confessions, silent yet profound, as the stars above watched over them.

When the first light of dawn crept over the horizon, painting the sky in hues of gold and pink, Emma and Alex remained in the garden, their hearts intertwined. The night had given way to a new day, but the secrets shared beneath the stars lingered, a testament to a bond that was becoming more unbreakable with each passing moment.

CHAPTER 2: DREAMS AND DESIRES

Unveiling Hidden Longings

The days began to blur into nights as Emma found herself lost in a world of dreams and desires, a world where reality and imagination intertwined seamlessly. Her encounters with Alex had opened a door within her, one that led to the hidden chambers of her heart where longings she had never dared to acknowledge lay in wait.

By day, Emma went through the motions of her routine, her mind often drifting back to the nights spent under the stars. The world around her seemed to pulse with a newfound vibrancy, every sight and sound infused with the magic of possibility. She found herself smiling at small things—a song on the radio, a gentle breeze, the laughter of strangers. Everything felt imbued with meaning, as if the universe itself was whispering secrets meant only for her.

Yet, it was in the quiet solitude of the night that her hidden longings truly emerged. As she lay in bed, her thoughts would inevitably drift to Alex, to the way his eyes crinkled when he smiled, the warmth of his touch, the soothing cadence of his voice. She found herself yearning for his presence, her heart beating to the rhythm of a melody only they could hear.

One evening, as the moon hung low in the sky, Emma decided to write. The words flowed from her like a river, each sentence a reflection of the emotions swirling within her. She wrote of dreams unfulfilled, of desires long suppressed, of a love that felt like it had been written in the stars. The act of writing was cathartic, a release of the emotions she had kept contained for so long.

As the pages filled with her thoughts, Emma realized something profound. Her dreams and desires were not burdens to be hidden away but gifts to be embraced. They were a part of her, a testament to the woman she was becoming—a woman unafraid to reach for the stars, to chase after what truly mattered.

The realization brought with it a sense of liberation, a freedom that had been elusive until now. Emma understood that to fully embrace her dreams, she needed to confront her fears, to let go of the doubts that held her back. It was a daunting prospect, but one she felt ready to face with Alex by her side.

Their next meeting was tinged with a newfound intensity, as if the air around them crackled with the energy of unspoken desires. Emma felt it in the way Alex looked at her, his gaze searching, as if trying to uncover the secrets she had yet to reveal.

"There's something different about you tonight," Alex observed, his voice a soft rumble that sent shivers down her spine.

Emma met his gaze, her heart laid bare in that moment. "I've been thinking a lot about dreams," she admitted, her voice steady. "About what I truly want."

Alex nodded, his expression thoughtful. "And what do you want, Emma?"

The question hung in the air, a challenge and an invitation all at once. Emma took a deep breath, the answer rising to the surface with clarity she hadn't expected. "I want to live fully, to embrace everything that life has to offer. I want to be with someone who makes me feel alive, who sees me for who I truly am."

A smile spread across Alex's face, his eyes alight with understanding. "And I want the same. I want to share those dreams with you, to explore them together."

The night wrapped around them, a cocoon of warmth and promise. Emma knew that the path ahead would not always be easy, but it was one she was eager to traverse. With Alex, she felt as if anything was possible, their shared dreams lighting the way forward.

Together, they stood on the precipice of something extraordinary, ready to leap into the unknown with open hearts and unbridled passion. The dreams and desires that had once been hidden were now unveiled, and with them, a love that promised to transcend the boundaries of night and day.

Whispers of the Heart

The nights grew longer as the seasons began to shift, their crisp chill a gentle reminder of time's passage. Yet, for Emma and Alex, the world seemed to exist in a perpetual twilight, a realm where their hearts spoke in whispers only they could hear.

Emma found herself drawn to the garden more often, its paths now familiar yet ever enchanting. It was here that she could hear the whispers of her heart most clearly, each rustling leaf and gentle breeze carrying secrets meant only for her. Her heart spoke in a language of its own, one that was as thrilling as it was terrifying.

On an evening when the moon hung like a silver pendant in the sky, Emma wandered through the garden with Alex by her side. The night was alive with the sound of crickets and the distant hoot of an owl, a symphony that played in the background of their silent conversation.

They walked in companionable silence, the bond between them deepening with each step. Alex seemed to sense her introspection, his presence a steady anchor amidst the swirling tide of her emotions.

"What's on your mind?" he asked, his voice a gentle prompt.

Emma paused, the weight of her thoughts pressing against her. "It's hard to explain," she admitted, her gaze fixed on the path ahead. "There's so much I want to say, but the words... they feel inadequate."

Alex nodded, his understanding a balm to her uncertainty. "Sometimes, words aren't enough," he mused. "It's what lies beneath them that truly matters."

His insight resonated with her, a reminder that the heart's whispers were often more powerful than mere words. Emma took a deep breath, summoning the courage to give voice to her feelings.

"I've never felt this way before," she confessed, her voice barely above a whisper. "Being with you feels like coming home, like I've found a part of myself I didn't know was missing."

Alex stopped, turning to face her. There was a vulnerability in his eyes, a reflection of the emotions she felt within. "I feel it too," he admitted, his voice steady yet filled with emotion. "It's as if we were meant to find each other, to share this journey."

The night seemed to hold its breath, the world around them fading into the background as they stood together, hearts laid bare. In that moment, Emma felt the whispers of her heart transform into a symphony, a harmony that resonated between them.

Alex reached for her hand, his touch a silent promise. "No matter where this leads, I'm here with you," he said, his words a pledge that echoed in the night.

Emma smiled, her heart full. She knew that the path ahead would not always be easy, but with Alex, she felt ready to face whatever came their way. Their hearts, now intertwined, beat in time with the rhythm of the night, a testament to a love that had been written in the stars.

As the night deepened, they continued to walk, their whispers a song carried on the wind. The garden, with its secrets and dreams, had become a sanctuary—a place where they could be truly themselves, where the whispers of their hearts could soar free.

Midnight Confessions

The clock ticked toward midnight, casting a spell of stillness over the world. The air was hushed, as if the earth itself paused to listen to the secrets that would be shared under the cover of darkness. Emma felt the weight of the moment, a quiet anticipation that settled in her bones as she and Alex returned once more to their cherished garden sanctuary.

The moon hung low, its silver light draping the landscape in a soft glow. Emma and Alex found their familiar spot by the ivy-clad bench, the place where so many of their revelations had emerged. Tonight, though, felt different—charged with an anticipation that promised a deeper unveiling of their souls.

As they sat, the cool stone grounding them, Emma took a deep breath, gathering her thoughts. The silence between them was comfortable, yet alive with the things left unsaid. She could feel the depth of her emotions, a river that had been steadily rising, now ready to overflow.

"There's something I need to tell you," Emma began, her voice calm yet firm. Her heart raced, but she knew that this was a moment she couldn't let pass.

Alex turned to her, his expression open and encouraging. "I'm listening."

Emma looked into his eyes, finding courage in the steady gaze that met hers. "I've been thinking a lot about what it means to be vulnerable," she admitted. "To truly let someone in."

Alex nodded, a silent understanding passing between them. "It's not easy," he acknowledged, his tone gentle. "But it's worth it."

Emma smiled, grateful for his patience. "I want you to know that you've become a part of me," she confessed, her words tumbling out with a fervor she hadn't anticipated. "I can't imagine my life without you in it."

The air seemed to shimmer with the weight of her confession, each word hanging between them like a delicate thread. Emma watched as Alex absorbed her words, his expression softening with something indescribable—a mix of relief, joy, and something deeper.

"I feel the same way," he said, his voice a quiet echo of her own emotions. "You've changed everything for me, Emma. Being with you... it's like seeing the world in color for the first time."

His confession, so raw and honest, filled her with an overwhelming sense of gratitude. They were two souls who had found each other against all odds, their paths converging in a dance of destiny that neither of them had anticipated.

In the quiet of the night, they spoke of their fears and hopes, their dreams and desires laid bare beneath the stars. Each confession was a step toward the future they were building together, a testament to the love that had grown from whispered secrets and midnight revelations.

As the first light of morning began to creep over the horizon, painting the sky with hues of pink and gold, Emma and Alex remained on the bench, their hearts intertwined. The night had given way to a new day, but the confessions shared in the midnight hour lingered, a promise of the journey yet to come.

Together, they watched as the dawn broke, their hands clasped tightly, ready to face whatever the world had in store. The garden, their sacred haven, bore witness to their vows— a love that transcended time and space, rooted in the confessions made under the watchful gaze of the moon.

CHAPTER 3: SHADOWS OF THE PAST

Echoes of Forgotten Love

The past has a way of lingering, weaving itself into the fabric of the present with threads both visible and hidden. For Emma, the echoes of forgotten love resided in quiet corners of her mind, casting shadows over her newfound happiness with Alex. It was a part of herself she had tried to leave behind, yet it whispered to her in moments of solitude, a reminder of wounds not yet fully healed.

The day was overcast, the sky a canvas of swirling gray as Emma found herself drawn to the garden once more. It was a place of solace, yet today, the beauty of the blooms seemed muted, as if reflecting her introspective mood. The weight of memories pressed down upon her, demanding acknowledgment.

Alex joined her, his presence a comforting balm against the chill that had settled within her. He sensed the shift in her demeanor, the unspoken tension that lay beneath the surface.

"Is everything alright?" he asked, concern lacing his voice.

Emma hesitated, choosing her words carefully. "It's just... there are things from my past," she began, her voice barely above a whisper. "Things I thought I'd moved on from, but they still haunt me."

Alex nodded, his understanding evident. "We all have our ghosts," he replied softly. "But you don't have to face them alone."

His words were a lifeline, a reminder that she no longer had to bear the burden on her own. Emma took a deep breath, the decision to share her past a weighty yet necessary choice.

"There was someone before," she admitted, her gaze distant. "Someone I thought I loved. But it ended, and I lost a part of myself in the process."

The confession hung in the air, a fragile truth that had been buried for too long. Emma felt the familiar sting of old wounds, yet alongside it, a sense of release.

Alex listened intently, his expression one of empathy. "It's hard to let go of something that once meant so much," he said gently. "But it doesn't define who you are now."

Emma met his gaze, finding strength in his unwavering support. "I know," she replied, her voice steadier. "But sometimes, it feels like a part of me is still trapped in the past, unable to fully embrace the present."

Alex reached for her hand, his touch both grounding and reassuring. "Then let's face it together," he suggested, his eyes filled with determination. "We'll turn those echoes into stepping stones, building something new."

His offer was a beacon of hope, a promise of healing and growth. Emma nodded, her heart swelling with gratitude for the love that had found her amidst the shadows.

As the afternoon wore on, they walked through the garden, their conversation a mix of shared stories and quiet reflection. Emma spoke of the love she had lost, the lessons learned and the scars that remained. Each word was a step toward healing, a reclaiming of her narrative.

In turn, Alex shared his own past, the experiences that had shaped him and the dreams that had carried him forward. The exchange was a weaving of their histories, a tapestry of understanding that strengthened the bond between them.

By the time the sun began to dip below the horizon, casting a warm glow over the garden, Emma felt a renewed sense of peace. The shadows of the past, though not entirely banished, had been rendered powerless by the light of shared understanding and love.

Together, they stood on the cusp of a new chapter, ready to embrace the future with open hearts and minds. The echoes of forgotten love would always be a part of Emma, but they no longer held sway over her. With Alex by her side, she felt ready to step into the light, leaving the shadows behind.

Unraveling Old Wounds

The garden that had become Emma and Alex's sanctuary now bore witness to a different kind of journey, one that delved into the depths of their pasts. It was a place of beauty, but also of reflection, where old wounds could be unraveled and understood.

As the evening settled in, the air was tinged with a crispness that hinted at the changing seasons. Emma and Alex walked side by side along the familiar paths, their hands intertwined, a silent promise of support and companionship. The conversation turned to the past, and with it, the scars that had yet to fully heal.

Emma paused near a cluster of sunflowers, their heads bowed as if in contemplation. She glanced at Alex, finding comfort in his steady presence. "I've been thinking a lot about what it means to truly heal," she admitted, her voice barely above the whisper of the wind.

Alex nodded, his expression one of understanding. "Healing isn't a linear process," he replied, his tone gentle. "It's more like a spiral, revisiting old wounds until they lose their power over us."

Emma considered his words, a sense of clarity emerging from the haze of introspection. "There are moments when I feel like I've moved on," she confessed. "But then something triggers a memory, and it's like I'm back at square one."

Alex squeezed her hand, a silent gesture of reassurance. "That's normal," he told her. "The past has a way of resurfacing, but it doesn't mean you're not healing."

Encouraged by his insight, Emma took a deep breath, ready to confront the memories that had lingered in the shadows. "There was a time when I lost myself in someone else's expectations," she began, her voice growing stronger. "I thought I had to be a certain way to be loved."

The admission was a release, a shedding of the weight she had carried for too long. Emma felt the sting of old wounds, yet alongside it, a sense of liberation.

"And now?" Alex prompted, his gaze steady and supportive.

Emma met his eyes, her heart swelling with newfound confidence. "Now I know that love should never demand we lose ourselves," she said, her voice firm. "With you, I feel like I can be genuinely me, flaws and all."

Alex smiled, his eyes reflecting the warmth of the setting sun. "That's all I ever wanted," he replied. "To love and be loved for who we truly are."

Their words hung in the air, a testament to the healing that had begun to take root. As they continued their walk, Emma felt the old wounds unraveling, their power diminished by the love and understanding she had found with Alex.

The garden, with its timeless beauty, seemed to embrace their journey, each step a move toward wholeness. They spoke of dreams and fears, of the future they were building together, and with each revelation, the past lost its grip.

By the time they reached the garden's edge, the first stars had begun to appear in the twilight sky. Emma felt a sense of peace, a quiet assurance that the path to healing was one she no longer had to walk alone.

As they stood side by side, the night unfolding around them, Emma knew that the old wounds, though not entirely forgotten, had been transformed. They were no longer chains but stepping stones, guiding her toward a future where love and authenticity reigned supreme.

Choices and Consequences

The evening was painted with a tapestry of stars, their light twinkling like distant promises in the vast expanse of the sky. Emma and Alex found themselves in the garden once more, the place that had become a witness to their unfolding story. Tonight, however, carried a different weight—a sense of gravity that accompanied the choices they knew they must soon make.

The path they walked was dappled with moonlight, the air filled with the heady scent of night-blooming jasmine. Emma's heart was a cacophony of emotions, a mix of hope and uncertainty as she considered the future that lay before them.

They reached a quiet alcove, the stone bench familiar and comforting. As they sat together, the silence stretched between them, pregnant with unspoken thoughts. Emma knew that the time had come to confront the decisions that would shape their journey forward.

"There's something I've been thinking about," Emma began, her voice steady yet tinged with apprehension. She turned to Alex, finding reassurance in the warmth of his gaze. "About us, and what it means to share a life together."

Alex nodded, his expression thoughtful. "I've been thinking about it too," he admitted. "Every choice we make has the power to change everything."

Emma knew the truth of his words, the weight of the choices they faced pressing upon her. They had come so far, unraveling old wounds and sharing their deepest dreams, but now they stood at a crossroads, where each path held its own set of consequences.

"I want to build a future with you," Emma confessed, her heart laid bare. "But it's terrifying to think about what we might have to give up or change to make that happen."

Alex reached for her hand, his touch both grounding and reassuring. "It's okay to be scared," he said gently. "But I believe that whatever we face, we can face it together."

His confidence was infectious, a balm to her fears. Emma felt a surge of gratitude for the man beside her, his unwavering support a constant in the shifting landscape of their lives.

"We'll have to make compromises," she acknowledged, her voice thoughtful. "But I'm willing to do that if it means being with you."

Alex smiled, his eyes reflecting the moonlight. "And I'm willing to do the same," he replied. "Love isn't about losing ourselves; it's about creating something new, something that's ours."

Their words hung in the air, a pact sealed beneath the stars. Emma knew that the path ahead would not always be easy, but the choices they made would be theirs, forged in love and understanding.

As they sat together, the garden a cocoon of tranquility, they spoke of the possibilities that awaited them. Each choice, though daunting, was a step toward the future they envisioned—a future where their lives were intertwined, a tapestry of shared experiences and dreams.

The night wore on, the stars bearing witness to their vows. Emma felt a sense of peace settle over her, a quiet assurance that whatever the consequences, they would face them together.

With Alex by her side, she felt ready to embrace the unknown, the choices and their consequences a testament to the love they had found. The garden, with its whispers of the past and promises of the future, was their sanctuary—a place where dreams were nurtured and love reigned supreme.

CHAPTER 4: STARLIT PROMISES

A Pledge Under the Moon

The night enveloped the garden in a gentle embrace, its serenity broken only by the soft murmur of leaves rustling in the breeze. Emma and Alex walked hand in hand, their steps in harmony, their hearts aligned with the rhythm of the universe. Tonight held a significance that was palpable, a moment where their dreams would be solidified in a starlit promise.

They found themselves beneath an ancient oak, its branches spreading wide like a protective canopy. The moon hung low in the sky, casting a silvery glow that transformed the world into a landscape of ethereal beauty. It was here, in this sacred space, that they paused, the weight of the moment pressing upon them like the warm embrace of an old friend.

Emma turned to Alex, her heart full, her mind clear. The journey they had embarked upon had led them to this point—each choice, each confession, each unraveling of the past a step toward the future they were now ready to claim.

"Do you remember when we first met in this garden?" Emma asked, her voice soft yet resonant with the echoes of their shared history.

Alex smiled, his eyes reflecting the moonlight. "How could I forget? It was as if the world conspired to bring us together, beneath these very stars."

Emma nodded, the memory vivid in her mind. The garden had been their sanctuary, a place where they had discovered not only each other but themselves. And now, it would be the backdrop for a pledge that would bind them in ways both seen and unseen.

"There's something I want to say," Emma continued, her voice steady with conviction. She took a deep breath, the words flowing from her heart. "You've changed my life, Alex. You've shown me what it means to be truly seen, to be loved for who I am. And I want to spend the rest of my life with you, creating new memories, new dreams."

Alex's gaze never wavered, his expression one of pure adoration. "Emma, you've given me hope and joy in ways I never imagined possible. I promise to stand by you, to support you, and to love you fiercely, no matter what life throws our way."

The air seemed to shimmer with the sincerity of their vows, a promise made under the watchful eyes of the stars. Emma felt the gravity of their words, a bond that transcended time and space, rooted in the love they had nurtured and grown.

As they stood beneath the oak, the world around them faded into the background, leaving only the two of them and the infinite possibilities that lay ahead. The garden, with its whispers of history and promises of the future, bore witness to their commitment, a sacred vow sealed beneath the starlit sky.

Emma felt a sense of peace envelop her, a certainty that whatever challenges and joys awaited, they would face them together. The starlit promises they made under the moon were a testament to the love they had found—a love that was as enduring as the night itself.

As the first light of dawn began to paint the horizon with hues of gold and pink, they remained beneath the oak, their hearts intertwined. Together, they watched as the world awoke, ready to embrace the future they had promised to share, their love a beacon guiding them forward.

Holding Onto Hope

The morning sun cast its golden light over the garden, breathing life into the world that Emma and Alex had come to cherish. The warmth of the new day was a welcome embrace, a reminder of the starlit promises they had made beneath the moon. Their commitment was a source of strength, a beacon that guided them as they navigated the uncharted waters of their shared future.

Yet, as with any journey, there were moments of doubt and uncertainty that crept in, casting shadows over the path they walked. Emma felt the weight of these moments, the whisper of fears that threatened to unravel the hope they had so carefully woven together.

One afternoon, as they strolled through the garden, Emma found herself reflecting on the fragility of hope. She turned to Alex, seeking solace in his presence. "Do you ever worry about what the future holds?" she asked, her voice tinged with trepidation.

Alex paused, considering her question. "Of course," he admitted, his tone thoughtful. "The future is full of unknowns, and that can be daunting. But I hold onto the belief that whatever comes, we'll face it together."

His words were a balm to her anxious heart, a reminder of the strength they drew from each other. Emma knew that hope was not a passive thing; it was an active choice, a commitment to see beyond the challenges that life inevitably presented.

As they continued their walk, the garden seemed to echo this sentiment, each bloom a testament to resilience and renewal. The vibrant colors and fragrant scents were a celebration of life, a reminder that beauty could thrive even in adversity.

Emma stopped by a bed of wildflowers, their petals dancing in the gentle breeze. "I want to hold onto that hope," she said, her voice steady with determination. "I want to believe that no matter what happens, we can create a future that's full of love and possibility."

Alex smiled, his expression one of unwavering support. "And we will," he assured her. "Hope is what fuels us, what keeps us moving forward even when the path seems uncertain."

His confidence was infectious, a spark that reignited her own sense of optimism. Emma felt a renewed sense of purpose, a desire to nurture the hope that had brought them together and would continue to sustain them.

The sun began to dip below the horizon, painting the sky with a palette of oranges and purples. As the day gave way to night, Emma and Alex returned to their familiar spot beneath the ancient oak. The tranquility of the garden enveloped them, a cocoon of peace and possibility.

As they sat together, the stars emerging one by one in the twilight sky, Emma felt a profound sense of gratitude. The journey they had embarked upon was not without its challenges, but it was one she faced with an open heart and a steadfast belief in the power of hope.

With Alex by her side, Emma knew that they could weather any storm. The garden, with its timeless beauty and whispers of the past, was a reminder that hope was a choice—one they made anew each day, a pledge to hold onto the light even when the world seemed dark.

As the night deepened, they spoke of dreams yet to be realized, of a future that awaited them with open arms. The hope they held was a promise, a testament to the love that had brought them this far and would continue to guide them on their journey together.

The Weight of a Promise

The days began to stretch into weeks, each one a testament to the life Emma and Alex were building together. Their starlit promises had become the foundation upon which they stood, a guiding light in the vast sea of their shared dreams and challenges. Yet, with each promise came a weight, an unspoken understanding of the responsibilities they had chosen to shoulder together.

One evening, as the sun dipped below the horizon, Emma found herself in the garden, her thoughts as restless as the wind that whispered through the trees. The weight of their commitments pressed upon her, a reminder of the delicate balance between love and expectation.

Alex joined her, his presence a familiar comfort in the twilight. He sensed the shift in her demeanor, the quiet introspection that had settled over her like a shadow. "You've been quiet today," he observed gently, his voice a soothing balm against the chill in the air.

Emma nodded, her gaze fixed on the horizon where the last sliver of daylight lingered. "I've been thinking about the promises we've made," she admitted, her voice thoughtful. "About what they mean for us, and how they shape our future."

Alex turned to face her, his expression open and understanding. "Promises can be heavy," he acknowledged, "but they're also what anchor us, what give us something to hold onto when everything else feels uncertain."

His words resonated with her, a reminder of the strength that lay within their shared vows. Emma took a deep breath, finding solace in the knowledge that they were navigating this journey together, each step a testament to their commitment.

"Sometimes, I worry about living up to those promises," Emma confessed, her vulnerability laid bare beneath the gathering dusk. "About being the person you need me to be."

Alex reached for her hand, his touch a gentle reassurance. "We chose each other for who we are, not who we think we should be," he reminded her. "Our promises aren't about perfection; they're about growth, about supporting each other through whatever comes our way."

Emma felt the weight of her concerns begin to lift, replaced by a renewed sense of purpose. Their promises were not chains binding them to an impossible ideal, but rather threads weaving a tapestry of shared experiences and dreams.

As the first stars appeared in the night sky, they continued their walk through the garden, the air alive with the scent of blooming jasmine. Emma felt a quiet contentment settle over her, a certainty that their love was strong enough to bear the weight of their promises.

They spoke of the future, of the dreams they held dear and the challenges they knew they would face. Each word was a reaffirmation of their commitment, a pledge to stand by each other through the ebbs and flows of life.

The garden, with its timeless beauty and whispers of history, was their sanctuary—a place where promises were made and kept, where love was nurtured and allowed to flourish. As they sat beneath the ancient oak, the world around them faded into the background, leaving only the two of them and the infinite possibilities that lay ahead.

Emma knew that the weight of a promise was not something to be feared, but embraced. It was a beacon guiding them forward, a testament to the love they had found and the life they were building together. With Alex by her side, she felt ready to face whatever the future held, their promises a light in the darkness, a reminder of the strength they drew from each other.

CHAPTER 5: THE DANCE OF FATE

Serendipitous Meetings

The tapestry of life is woven with threads of chance and choice, a delicate dance where fate plays its unpredictable tune. For Emma and Alex, the garden had always been a stage for their unfolding story, but the world beyond its boundaries held surprises that neither of them could anticipate.

It was a sunny afternoon when Emma decided to venture into town, her thoughts buzzing with the excitement of a new project she hoped to start. As she strolled through the bustling market square, the air filled with the vibrant sounds of life, she felt a sense of freedom that she hadn't experienced in a while. Her heart was light, her mind open to the possibilities that lay ahead.

Amidst the colorful stalls and lively chatter, Emma's attention was drawn to a small corner café, its inviting aroma of freshly brewed coffee wafting through the air. She decided to indulge herself, stepping inside and finding a cozy spot by the window.

As she settled down with her cup, Emma's gaze wandered over the familiar scene outside—the ebb and flow of people going about their day, each one a part of the intricate dance of life. It was then that she noticed a familiar face amidst the crowd, a figure she hadn't seen in years but recognized instantly.

It was Daniel, an old friend from her university days, someone who had once been an integral part of her life. The sight of him stirred a mix of emotions, a reminder of a chapter she had long since closed but had never truly forgotten.

Emma hesitated for a moment, uncertainty clouding her thoughts. But fate, it seemed, had its own plans. Before she could decide on her next move, Daniel turned and caught her eye, a look of surprised recognition lighting up his features.

He waved, a smile breaking across his face, and Emma felt the pull of serendipity guiding her forward. She rose from her seat, weaving through the bustling café to greet him.

"Emma! I can't believe it's you," Daniel exclaimed, his voice warm with genuine delight. "It's been too long."

Emma smiled, the initial awkwardness melting away in the warmth of his welcome. "It has been. I didn't expect to run into you here."

They settled into a comfortable conversation, reminiscing about old times and catching up on the years that had passed. Daniel spoke of his travels and the unexpected turns his life had taken, while Emma shared her journey, the challenges and joys she had encountered along the way.

As they talked, Emma felt a sense of closure, a realization that the past no longer held sway over her present. The dance of fate, with its serendipitous meetings and unexpected encounters, had brought her to this moment, reaffirming the choices she had made and the path she had chosen.

Later, as she made her way back to the garden, Emma reflected on the encounter. It was as if the universe had conspired to remind her of the beauty in life's unpredictability, the magic that lay in moments of chance.

When she returned home, Alex was waiting for her, his presence a constant source of comfort and love. She recounted her day, the unexpected meeting with Daniel, and the sense of fulfillment it had brought her.

Alex listened with interest, his eyes reflecting the understanding and support that defined their relationship. "It sounds like it was meant to happen," he mused, his voice thoughtful. "A reminder that life has a way of bringing us exactly what we need, even when we least expect it."

Emma nodded, her heart full. The dance of fate, with its twists and turns, had brought her to this place of peace and contentment. With Alex by her side, she felt ready to embrace whatever surprises life had in store, knowing that each step in the dance was a part of the journey they shared together.

The Pull of Destiny

The world seemed to hold its breath as Emma stood at the threshold of her future, the pull of destiny a palpable force that guided her steps. It was an ordinary day, yet she felt the undercurrent of something extraordinary, a whisper of change that lingered in the corners of her consciousness.

The routine of daily life unfolded around her, each moment seemingly mundane yet charged with significance. Emma found herself drawn to the garden once more, the place where so much of her story with Alex had taken shape. The familiar paths and blooming flowers were a comfort, a reminder of the journey they had embarked upon together.

As she wandered through the garden, Emma felt a deep sense of connection to the world around her, as if the very earth beneath her feet was alive with possibility. The pull of destiny was a gentle tug, urging her to remain open to the unforeseen, to trust in the unfolding of her life's narrative.

Alex joined her, his presence a reassuring anchor in the sea of uncertainty. He too seemed attuned to the subtle shifts in the air, his gaze thoughtful as they walked side by side.

"Have you ever felt like you're on the brink of something?" Emma asked, her voice soft yet filled with curiosity.

Alex nodded, his expression contemplative. "I think we all feel that way sometimes," he replied. "Like there's a path waiting for us, if only we have the courage to follow it."

Emma considered his words, a sense of clarity emerging from the haze of anticipation. "It's like the universe is nudging us in a certain direction," she mused. "Encouraging us to take that leap of faith."

The conversation lingered in the air, a testament to their shared understanding and the bond that had grown between them. Emma felt a renewed sense of purpose, a desire to embrace the unknown with open arms and an open heart.

The day unfolded with a quiet grace, each moment a dance between the ordinary and the extraordinary. Emma and Alex spoke of dreams and aspirations, of the life they were building and the adventures that awaited them.

In the golden light of afternoon, they paused by a cluster of lavender, the fragrant blooms swaying gently in the breeze. Emma closed her eyes, breathing in the scent and allowing the pull of destiny to wash over her.

When she opened her eyes, she turned to Alex, her heart full. "Whatever comes, I know we'll face it together," she said, her voice steady with conviction.

Alex smiled, his eyes alight with the same sense of certainty. "Together, we can handle anything," he agreed. "The future is ours to shape."

As the sun began its descent, painting the sky with hues of orange and pink, Emma felt a profound sense of peace. The pull of destiny, with its whispers of promise and possibility, was a guiding force in their lives, a reminder that they were exactly where they were meant to be.

With Alex by her side, Emma felt ready to step into the unknown, to embrace the adventures and challenges that lay ahead. The garden, with its timeless beauty and echoes of the past, was a sanctuary—a place where dreams were born and destiny awaited. Together, they walked forward, hand in hand, their hearts open to the journey that lay before them.

Crossroads of the Heart

The path of love is often lined with choices, each decision a crossroads where the heart must navigate its own truth. For Emma and Alex, the journey had been filled with moments of clarity and doubt, the pull of destiny guiding them yet leaving room for uncertainty. Now, as they stood at a metaphorical crossroad, the weight of their choices pressed upon them with an intensity that could not be ignored.

The morning dawned with a crispness in the air, a subtle reminder of the changing seasons. Emma awoke with a sense of anticipation, the kind that heralds a day of significance. She knew that the time had come for a conversation that could alter the course of their lives together.

After breakfast, they retreated to the garden, their sanctuary amidst the chaos of the world. The ancient oak stood sentinel, its branches casting dappled shadows that danced upon the ground. Emma took a deep breath, the serenity of the setting giving her the courage she needed.

"Alex," she began, her voice calm yet resolute. "There's something we need to talk about. A decision we need to make."

Alex regarded her with a steady gaze, his expression open and attentive. "I'm listening," he replied, his voice a reassuring balm.

Emma hesitated for a moment, gathering her thoughts. "We've talked about the future, about our hopes and dreams," she continued. "But I think it's time we decide where we're heading, what we truly want from our life together."

The words hung in the air, charged with the gravity of the moment. It was a conversation that had been brewing beneath the surface, a necessary step in their journey.

Alex nodded, his demeanor thoughtful. "I've been thinking about it too," he admitted. "About what it means to build a life together, and the sacrifices we might need to make."

Emma appreciated his honesty, his willingness to face the complexities of their relationship head-on. "I want to make sure we're on the same path," she said, her voice earnest. "That we're moving forward with purpose and intention."

Their words wove a tapestry of understanding, each thread a testament to their shared commitment. Emma felt the crossroads before them, the myriad of choices that lay in wait, each one a potential turning point in their lives.

As they walked through the garden, they spoke of their dreams, their values, and the vision they held for their future. The conversation was a dance, a delicate balance of give and take, where each offered their heart and listened with an open mind.

Emma felt a sense of clarity emerging from the dialogue, a realization that the crossroads of the heart was not a place of fear but of opportunity. It was a chance to align their paths, to forge a future that honored both individuality and partnership.

By the time the sun began its descent, casting a warm glow over the garden, Emma and Alex had reached a consensus. Their choices were not final, but they were grounded in love and understanding, a promise to support each other as they navigated the unknown.

As they stood beneath the ancient oak, the world around them fading into the twilight, Emma felt a renewed sense of hope. The crossroads of the heart, with its challenges and possibilities, was a journey they would face together, hand in hand, their love a guiding light in the ever-unfolding tapestry of their lives.

CHAPTER 6: TWILIGHT REVELATIONS

Truths in the Night

The evening descended upon the garden with a gentle hush, the sky painted in deep indigos and purples as twilight cast its spell. Emma and Alex found solace in the tranquility that surrounded them, the world held in a brief pause between day and night. There was something about the darkness that invited introspection, a quiet space where truths could emerge, unbidden and unguarded.

As the stars began to prick the sky with their ancient light, Emma felt a stirring within her, a desire to unearth the truths that had remained hidden in the corners of her heart. The crossroads they had navigated earlier had left her contemplative, and she knew that the time had come to share her innermost thoughts.

They settled onto the stone bench beneath the ancient oak, the cool night air wrapping around them like a familiar embrace. Alex sat beside her, his presence a steady anchor amidst the currents of uncertainty.

"Alex," Emma began, her voice a quiet thread in the tapestry of night sounds. "There's something I've been meaning to tell you, something I've been holding onto for a while."

He turned to her, his expression open and inviting. "You can tell me anything," he assured her, his eyes reflecting the sincerity of his words.

Emma took a deep breath, her heart steadying as she prepared to lay bare the truths she had kept close for too long. "I've always believed that vulnerability is a strength," she said, her voice gaining confidence. "But there are parts of my past that I've struggled to share, even with myself."

Alex listened intently, his gaze unwavering. "Whatever it is, we'll face it together," he promised, his hand finding hers in a gesture of solidarity.

Encouraged by his unwavering support, Emma continued. "There were times in my life when I felt lost, like I was drifting without a sense of purpose. Meeting you changed everything, but I still carry those fears of losing myself again."

The admission hung in the air, a truth illuminated by the soft glow of the moon. Emma felt a sense of release, the burden of secrecy lifted from her shoulders.

Alex's response was immediate, his voice filled with warmth and understanding. "We all carry parts of our past with us," he said gently. "But they don't define us. It's what we choose to do with those experiences that shapes who we are."

Emma felt her heart swell with gratitude for the man beside her, his compassion a balm to her fears. "Thank you for understanding," she murmured, her voice filled with emotion. "I want to move forward without those shadows holding me back."

Their conversation lingered in the night air, a testament to the strength of their bond and the power of truth. Emma realized that sharing her fears had not only brought her closer to Alex but had also allowed her to embrace her own resilience.

As the night deepened, they spoke of dreams yet to be realized, of the life they were crafting together. The garden, with its whispers of history and echoes of the past, was a sanctuary—a place where truths were revealed and love was nurtured.

Emma felt a profound sense of peace settle over her, a quiet certainty that the truths of the night had woven them closer together. With Alex by her side, she felt ready to embrace the future, their shared revelations a testament to the depth of their connection.

As they sat beneath the stars, the world around them softened by the gentle embrace of night, Emma knew that the truths they had uncovered were not burdens but stepping stones. Together, they would continue to navigate the tapestry of their lives, guided by the light of love and the courage to face whatever lay ahead.

The Unspoken Bond

The days that followed their twilight revelations were imbued with a new sense of understanding. Emma and Alex found themselves moving through life with a deeper awareness of the unspoken bond that connected them. It was as if the truths they had unearthed beneath the stars had woven an invisible thread between their hearts, strengthening their connection in ways words alone never could.

The garden, their cherished refuge, became a place where silence spoke volumes. Each rustle of leaves, each whisper of the wind carried meaning, communicating the nuances of their shared journey. Emma found solace in these quiet moments, where the world seemed to pause and allow them to simply be.

One afternoon, as the sun cast a warm glow over the garden, Emma found herself reflecting on the nature of their bond. It was a connection that transcended the need for constant verbal affirmation, a silent understanding that resonated in the spaces between their conversations.

Alex joined her, his presence a comforting familiarity. They walked side by side, the crunch of gravel underfoot a rhythmic accompaniment to their thoughts. Emma felt the urge to express the depth of her gratitude, to articulate the significance of what they shared.

"Isn't it strange how some things don't need to be said?" she mused aloud, her voice a gentle ripple in the afternoon air. "How we can understand each other without speaking?"

Alex nodded, his gaze thoughtful. "It's like a dance," he replied, "where each step is guided by instinct rather than instruction. We just know."

Emma smiled, appreciating the poetry in his words. "I've never experienced anything like it before," she confessed. "This connection we have—it's rare and precious."

Their conversation flowed effortlessly, an exchange that required no embellishment. Emma felt the weight of the unspoken bond, a presence that was both grounding and liberating. It was a reminder that love was not always loud; sometimes, it was found in the quiet moments, in the shared glances and subtle gestures that spoke volumes.

As they paused by the pond, its surface a mirror reflecting the sky, Emma felt a surge of emotion. The simplicity of their bond was its greatest strength, a foundation built on trust, respect, and an unwavering commitment to one another.

Alex turned to her, his eyes alight with the same sentiment. "I'm grateful for this," he said softly, "for the way we understand each other without having to explain everything. It feels… easy."

Emma nodded, her heart full. "It does," she agreed. "And I think that's what makes it so special. We don't have to try; we just are."

Their words were a quiet acknowledgment of the journey they had traveled, a testament to the bond that had grown between them. Emma realized that the unspoken bond was not a mystery to be solved, but a gift to be cherished—a rare alignment of hearts and minds that transcended the need for constant validation.

As the sun dipped lower in the sky, casting long shadows across the garden, they continued their walk, content in the knowledge that their connection was strong and enduring. Emma felt a profound sense of peace, a certainty that the unspoken bond was a guiding light in their lives, illuminating the path they walked together.

With each step, Emma and Alex embraced the beauty of their silent understanding, knowing that the bond they shared would continue to grow and evolve, a testament to the love that had brought them together and the journey that lay ahead.

Unveiling the Mask

The quiet strength of their unspoken bond had carried Emma and Alex through the ebb and flow of their days. Yet, beneath the surface, lay layers of self that each had yet to reveal. The garden, their sanctuary and stage for the unfolding of their lives, seemed to whisper of secrets waiting to be unveiled.

It was an afternoon of scattered sunlight and gentle breezes when Emma felt the stirrings of something deeper within her. The shadows of the past, long-kept and seldom acknowledged, began to press against the edges of her consciousness. She knew it was time to confront the parts of herself that she had kept hidden, to unveil the mask she had worn for so long.

As she wandered through the garden, Emma felt the weight of her own history, the memories that had shaped her yet remained unspoken. She realized that true intimacy required vulnerability, a willingness to reveal the facets of oneself that lay beneath the surface.

Later, as they sat beneath the ancient oak, Alex sensed her contemplative mood. His presence was an invitation, a gentle encouragement to share the thoughts that lingered in the shadows.

"Emma," he began, his voice a soft invitation, "I can see something's on your mind. You know you can tell me anything, right?"

His words were a lifeline, a reminder of the trust they had built. Emma took a deep breath, gathering the courage to speak her truth. "There are parts of my past that I haven't shared," she admitted, her voice steady but tinged with emotion. "Things I've hidden even from myself, because facing them felt too difficult."

Alex nodded, his expression one of understanding and patience. "We all wear masks at times," he replied, "but we don't have to wear them forever."

Emma felt a surge of gratitude for his acceptance, the unwavering support that gave her the strength to continue. "I want to share this with you," she said, her voice gaining confidence. "To show you the parts of me that are less polished, less certain."

The conversation flowed like a river, each word a step towards unveiling the mask she had worn. Emma spoke of her fears, her insecurities, the moments of doubt that had colored her past. She revealed the dreams she had once set aside, the aspirations she had kept close to her heart.

Alex listened with empathy, his presence a steady anchor amidst the tide of emotions. He responded not with judgment, but with a quiet understanding that enveloped her like a warm embrace.

"Thank you for sharing this with me," he said softly, his eyes filled with compassion. "I'm here for you, every step of the way. You're not alone."

The weight of her confession lifted, replaced by a sense of liberation. Emma realized that unveiling the mask was not an act of weakness, but a brave step towards authenticity—a way to deepen the connection they shared.

As the sun dipped below the horizon, casting a golden glow over the garden, Emma felt a profound sense of peace. The mask she had worn was no longer necessary, the truths she had unveiled a testament to the strength of their bond.

Together, they stood beneath the ancient oak, the world around them bathed in the soft light of dusk. Emma knew that the unveiling of her mask was a new beginning, a chance to embrace her true self with Alex by her side.

The garden, with its timeless beauty and whispers of history, bore witness to their journey. Emma felt ready to step into the future, her heart open and her spirit free, knowing that the path ahead was one they would navigate together, hand in hand.

CHAPTER 7: LOVE'S LABYRINTH

Navigating the Maze

The journey of love is seldom a straight path; it twists and turns like a labyrinth, each corner revealing new challenges and unexpected joys. For Emma and Alex, the unveiling of masks had opened doors to deeper understanding, yet it also laid bare the complexities of their hearts. The garden, ever a symbol of their evolving story, echoed with the mysteries of love's labyrinth.

The morning was bright with promise, the air crisp with the scent of blooming roses. Emma found herself drawn to the garden's winding paths, a desire to explore the depths of her emotions guiding her steps. The labyrinth of love was a terrain she was learning to navigate, each twist and turn a lesson in trust and patience.

As she walked, Emma pondered the intricacies of their relationship. The unveiling had been a revelation, a pivotal moment that deepened their connection. But it also brought to light the challenges inherent in merging two lives, two histories, into one cohesive journey.

Alex joined her in the garden, his presence a comforting constant amidst the shifting tides of emotion. Together, they wandered through the maze of hedges, their conversation flowing with the ease of a shared understanding.

"Do you ever feel like we're navigating a maze?" Emma asked, her voice thoughtful. "Like there's always something new to discover, but also something to overcome?"

Alex chuckled softly, his eyes reflecting a mixture of amusement and agreement. "Love is definitely a maze," he replied. "But it's one I'm glad to be exploring with you. I think the twists and turns are what make it interesting."

Emma smiled, appreciating his perspective. "I suppose that's true," she conceded. "Each challenge is an opportunity to learn, to grow closer."

Their conversation meandered through the complexities of love, touching on the moments of joy and the trials they had faced. Emma realized that the maze was not a barrier, but a journey—a testament to the resilience and adaptability of their bond.

As they reached a clearing, Emma paused, taking in the beauty of the garden around them. The sunlight filtered through the leaves, casting intricate patterns on the ground, a reminder of the labyrinthine nature of their journey.

"Sometimes I think the maze is more about the journey than the destination," she mused. "It's about finding our way together, no matter how convoluted the path might seem."

Alex nodded, his expression one of thoughtful agreement. "And as long as we keep moving forward, keep communicating, we'll find our way through it," he added. "Together."

Emma felt a sense of peace settle over her, the reassurance of their shared commitment a guiding light in the labyrinth. The path of love, with its myriad twists and turns, was a testament to their shared journey—a journey marked by growth, understanding, and unwavering support.

As they continued their walk, Emma realized that the maze of love was not something to be feared, but embraced. Each step was a dance of discovery, each twist a chance to deepen their connection. With Alex by her side, she felt ready to navigate the labyrinth, confident in their ability to face whatever challenges lay ahead.

The garden, with its timeless beauty and whispers of history, stood witness to their journey. Emma knew that as they continued through love's labyrinth, their bond would only grow stronger, the path ahead illuminated by the light of their shared dreams and the strength of their hearts.

Torn Between Two Worlds

The labyrinth of love had taught Emma and Alex the art of navigation, but the path ahead was about to present them with a choice that would test the very fabric of their relationship. As they stood at the precipice of a crossroads, Emma found herself torn between two worlds, each pulling her in a different direction. The garden, their sanctuary, seemed to hum with the tension of her internal struggle.

Emma's world had always been one of creativity and dreams, a realm where ideas flourished and possibilities were endless. Yet, the pull of another world—a world of stability and responsibility—beckoned her with its promise of security and certainty. It was a choice that weighed heavily on her heart, a decision that felt both inevitable and impossible.

One evening, as the sun dipped below the horizon, casting long shadows over the garden, Emma found herself lost in thought. She sat beneath the ancient oak, the weight of her dilemma pressing upon her. The two worlds, each with its own allure and demands, seemed to stretch endlessly before her, and she felt caught in the middle, unsure of which path to choose.

Alex, attuned to the changes in her demeanor, joined her beneath the tree. His presence was a balm, a reminder that she was not alone in her struggle. "Emma," he said softly, "I can see something's been on your mind. Do you want to talk about it?"

Emma hesitated, the words tangled in her throat. But the sincerity in his eyes, the unwavering support in his voice, gave her the courage to speak. "I feel like I'm being pulled in two directions," she confessed. "On one hand, there's the life I've always dreamed of—full of creativity and passion. On the other, there's a path that offers stability and security, something I've never really had."

Alex listened, his expression one of understanding and empathy. "It's not easy, feeling torn between two worlds," he acknowledged. "But whatever you choose, I'll support you. We'll find a way through it together."

His words were a lifeline, a reminder that she didn't have to face this decision alone. Emma felt a wave of gratitude wash over her, the knowledge that their bond was strong enough to weather the storms of uncertainty.

"I'm afraid of losing myself," she admitted, her voice a whisper in the twilight. "Afraid that choosing one path means giving up the other."

Alex reached for her hand, his touch a grounding force. "You don't have to choose right now," he reassured her. "Take the time you need. Your dreams and ambitions are part of who you are, and I wouldn't want you to give them up."

Emma felt a sense of relief, the pressure of her decision easing in the face of his unwavering support. She realized that the choice was not about abandoning one world for another, but about finding a balance that honored both her dreams and her reality.

As the stars began to emerge, twinkling in the night sky like distant beacons, Emma felt a renewed sense of clarity. The decision she faced was not insurmountable; it was a journey to be navigated with care and consideration. With Alex by her side, she felt ready to explore both worlds, to find a way to weave them together into the tapestry of her life.

The garden, with its timeless beauty and whispers of history, bore witness to her resolve. Emma knew that as she stood at the crossroads of her heart, she was not alone. Together, she and Alex would navigate the path ahead, their love a guiding light through the uncertainty of the worlds that lay before them.

The Journey Within

The garden, with its labyrinth of paths and secrets, had always been a place of solace for Emma. Yet as she stood at the crossroads of her life, she realized that the journey she needed to embark upon was not one of external exploration, but an inward odyssey—a journey within her own heart and mind.

The decision to navigate between two worlds had left her feeling adrift, her sense of identity fragmented by the choices before her. She knew that to find clarity, she must first delve into the depths of her own soul, to understand the desires and fears that shaped her path.

One morning, as the first light of dawn kissed the horizon, Emma found herself drawn to the garden once more. The air was crisp and filled with the promise of a new day, a canvas upon which she could begin to paint the contours of her inner journey.

Emma settled onto the stone bench beneath the ancient oak, its branches stretching toward the sky like arms reaching for the divine. She closed her eyes, allowing the sounds and scents of the garden to envelop her, grounding her in the present moment.

In the quiet sanctuary of her mind, Emma began to unravel the tapestry of her thoughts. She reflected on the dreams that had guided her through life, the passions that set her soul ablaze. She considered the fears that had crept into her heart, the doubts that whispered of inadequacy and uncertainty.

As she journeyed deeper into her own consciousness, Emma felt the layers of her identity begin to peel away, revealing the core of who she truly was. It was a process both exhilarating and terrifying, a dance between vulnerability and empowerment.

Through this introspection, Emma discovered that her dreams and desires were not mutually exclusive. The creativity and passion that had always defined her could coexist with the stability and security she yearned for. It was not a matter of choosing between two worlds, but of integrating them into a harmonious whole.

With each revelation, Emma felt a sense of liberation, the shackles of indecision falling away. The journey within had illuminated the path forward, a road that honored both her artistic spirit and her practical aspirations.

When she finally opened her eyes, the garden was bathed in the soft glow of morning light. Emma felt a profound sense of peace, her heart lightened by the clarity she had found within herself.

Alex appeared, his presence a comforting constant in the ever-shifting landscape of her life. He joined her beneath the oak, his gaze filled with curiosity and warmth.

"How are you feeling?" he asked, his voice gentle and inviting.

Emma smiled, the serenity of her journey reflected in her eyes. "Lighter," she replied. "I've realized that the path isn't about choosing one world over another. It's about embracing all parts of myself, finding a way to bring them together."

Alex nodded, his expression one of understanding. "I knew you'd find your way," he said softly. "You've always had a remarkable strength within you."

His words were a balm, reinforcing the newfound clarity she had discovered. Emma knew that as she continued her journey, both within and without, she was not alone. With Alex by her side, she felt ready to face whatever challenges lay ahead, confident in the knowledge that her inner journey had prepared her for the world beyond.

Together, they rose from the bench, the garden around them a testament to the beauty and resilience of their shared journey. Emma felt a sense of gratitude for the path she had traveled, both the inner and the outer, knowing that each step had brought her closer to the woman she was meant to be.

CHAPTER 8: THE LIGHT OF LOVE

A Beacon in the Darkness

The journey within had offered Emma a newfound clarity, illuminating the path she was meant to tread. Yet, as with any path, shadows lingered at the edges, threatening to obscure the way forward. It was during these moments of doubt and uncertainty that Emma discovered the true power of love—a light that could pierce even the darkest corners of the heart.

The garden, their eternal refuge, was alive with the vibrant hues of early summer. The air was fragrant with the scent of jasmine, and the gentle hum of bees filled the spaces between the rustling leaves. Emma and Alex found themselves drawn to this sanctuary, a place where love had always flourished amidst the trials of their journey.

One evening, as twilight descended like a velvet curtain, Emma felt the familiar tendrils of doubt creep into her mind. The decisions she faced, the balance she sought between worlds, weighed heavily on her spirit. It was a darkness she had encountered before, yet this time, she was determined to face it with the strength she had nurtured within.

Alex sensed her unease, the subtle shifts in her demeanor speaking volumes. He took her hand, his touch a grounding force that anchored her to the present. They walked together along the garden's winding paths, the soft glow of lanterns casting pools of light upon the ground.

"Emma," Alex began, his voice a gentle balm against the night, "I can see the shadows in your eyes. What's weighing on you?"

Emma paused, her gaze drawn to the flickering lanterns, their light a metaphor for the love that had guided her through the darkest times. "It's just… sometimes the journey feels overwhelming," she admitted. "Even with all the clarity I've found, there are moments when the doubts return."

Alex nodded, his expression one of empathy and understanding. "We all have those moments," he replied. "But remember, you're not alone. Love is the light that guides us through the darkness."

His words resonated within her, a reminder of the strength they had built together. Emma realized that the light of love was not just an abstract concept, but a tangible force—one that had the power to illuminate the path ahead, no matter how obscured it might seem.

As they continued their walk, Emma felt the warmth of Alex's presence envelop her, the love they shared a beacon in the encroaching darkness. She understood that while doubts might linger, they did not define her journey. The light of love was ever-present, a constant source of guidance and comfort.

They stopped by the pond, its surface a mirror reflecting the stars above. Emma felt a surge of gratitude for the man beside her, for the love that had stood unwavering against the trials they had faced. "Thank you for being my light," she said softly, her voice barely above a whisper.

Alex smiled, his eyes alight with the same warmth that filled her heart. "And you are mine," he replied, his words a promise and a testament to their shared journey.

In that moment, surrounded by the beauty and tranquility of the garden, Emma felt the shadows recede, replaced by the gentle glow of love's light. She knew that the path ahead would not always be easy, but with Alex by her side, she was ready to face whatever lay in wait.

Together, they stood beneath the stars, the garden around them a silent witness to their enduring bond. Emma understood that the light of love was not just a beacon in the darkness, but a guiding force in their lives—a reminder that no matter how twisted the path might become, they would always find their way back to each other.

Embracing the Dawn

The dawn of a new day crept over the horizon, casting its golden light upon the garden that had become the backdrop to Emma and Alex's unfolding story. The night's shadows had retreated, leaving behind a world washed in the soft hues of morning—a symbol of renewal and hope. It was a day that promised new beginnings, a chance to embrace the future with open hearts and unyielding optimism.

Emma awoke with a sense of anticipation, the kind of energy that accompanies the first light of day. The clarity she had discovered on her inward journey mingled with the steadfast light of love, creating a harmonious symphony of resolve and warmth. Today felt different, imbued with the promise of possibilities waiting to be explored.

Stepping into the garden, she found Alex already there, his silhouette framed by the rising sun. The air was crisp, carrying with it the scent of dew-kissed earth and blooming flowers. It was a morning alive with potential, each moment a step toward the day that lay ahead.

"There's something magical about the dawn," Emma mused as she joined Alex. "It's like the world is waking up to endless possibilities."

Alex nodded, his smile reflecting the light that danced around them. "Every dawn is a new beginning," he agreed. "A chance to start fresh, to embrace whatever comes our way."

Their words were a quiet affirmation of the journey they had traveled and the path that stretched before them. The garden, with its timeless beauty and history, seemed to echo their sentiments, its vibrant colors a testament to the resilience and renewal of life.

As they walked, Emma felt a sense of liberation, a readiness to step into the future with confidence and grace. The journey within had revealed her true self, and the light of love had illuminated the path. Now, she felt poised to embrace the dawn, to welcome the adventures and challenges that awaited them.

They paused by the pond, the water's surface shimmering with the reflections of the awakening sky. It was a place of tranquility, a reminder of the peace they had found within themselves and each other.

"Whatever happens," Emma said, her voice filled with quiet determination, "I know we'll face it together. The dawn is ours to embrace."

Alex took her hand, his touch a promise of unwavering support and partnership. "Together," he echoed, his words a vow and a celebration of their shared journey.

In the gentle light of morning, Emma felt her heart swell with gratitude and love. The dawn was not just a beginning; it was a continuation of the story they had crafted together, a testament to the strength and beauty of their bond.

As they stood side by side, the garden around them alive with the whispers of the past and the promise of the future, Emma knew that they were ready to face whatever lay ahead. With the dawn as their guide, they would navigate the twists and turns of life's labyrinth, their love a constant beacon illuminating the way.

Together, they embraced the dawn, the world a canvas upon which they would paint the next chapter of their lives—a story of love, resilience, and the endless possibilities of a new day.

A Love Reborn

The garden, a witness to the seasons of Emma and Alex's love, now flourished in the full bloom of summer. Each petal and leaf seemed to sing of renewal, echoing the transformation that had taken place within their hearts. It was a time of rebirth, and their love, once tested and refined, was blossoming anew—stronger and more vibrant than ever before.

Emma felt it in the way they moved through their days, a seamless dance of understanding and shared purpose. The doubts and shadows that once lingered at the edges had given way to a profound sense of peace and certainty. Their love had been reborn, forged in the crucible of experience and discovery.

One afternoon, as the sun painted the garden in warm, golden hues, Emma and Alex found themselves drawn to their favorite spot beneath the ancient oak. Its branches stretched above them like a protective canopy, a symbol of the enduring strength and shelter they had found in each other.

Emma leaned against the tree, her gaze wandering over the familiar landscape that had become a sanctuary for their hearts. "It's amazing how much we've grown," she reflected, her voice a soft melody in the summer air. "Our love feels... different. More alive."

Alex nodded, his smile a mirror of her own contentment. "It's like we've found a new rhythm," he agreed. "One that's in tune with who we are now, after everything we've been through."

Their conversation flowed with the ease of a well-loved song, each word an affirmation of the journey that had brought them to this moment. Emma realized that their love, once fragile and untested, had transformed into something enduring and resilient—a love reborn from the trials and triumphs they had faced together.

As they sat in the dappled shade, Emma felt a sense of gratitude wash over her. The journey had not been without its challenges, but it was those very obstacles that had strengthened their bond, deepening the connection that anchored them to one another.

"Do you remember when we first started this journey?" Emma mused, a smile playing at her lips. "I had no idea just how much we would grow together."

Alex chuckled, his eyes sparkling with affection. "I remember," he said fondly. "And I wouldn't change a single moment. Every step brought us here."

The garden, alive with the sounds of summer, seemed to agree, its vibrant colors a testament to the life and love that flourished within its bounds. Emma felt the warmth of the sun on her skin, a reminder of the light that had guided them through even the darkest times.

In that moment, beneath the ancient oak, Emma understood that their love was not just a singular emotion, but a living, breathing entity—one that had been reborn and renewed with each passing day. It was a love that celebrated their individuality while embracing the unity they had forged together.

As the afternoon sun cast long shadows across the garden, Emma and Alex rose to continue their walk, hand in hand. Their love, once a seed of possibility, had grown into a mighty tree, its roots deep and unshakable.

Together, they stepped forward into the future, their hearts alight with the promise of new adventures and shared dreams. In the garden, their love had been reborn, and with each step, they nurtured it, allowing it to flourish and thrive—an everlasting testament to the power of love and the beauty of a journey shared.

CHAPTER 9: MOONLIGHT AND MEMORIES

A Night to Remember

The garden had always been a place of solace and growth for Emma and Alex, but tonight it held a special magic. The moon hung high in the sky, casting its silvery glow over the world below, turning the familiar paths and trees into a landscape of dreams. It was a night for memories, for reflection, and for celebrating the journey they had traveled together.

As they stepped into the garden, the cool night air wrapped around them like a gentle embrace. Emma felt a thrill of anticipation, the kind that comes with knowing something unforgettable is about to unfold. The moonlight danced across the leaves, painting the world in shades of silver and shadow, as if the garden itself was a stage set for a night to remember.

They wandered through the paths, their footsteps soft on the dew-kissed grass. Each turn and corner seemed to whisper of the moments they had shared, the laughter and tears that had woven the tapestry of their love. It was as if the garden held their memories, safeguarding them against the passage of time.

Emma paused by the pond, its surface a mirror reflecting the moon's luminescent face. She turned to Alex, her heart full of the journey that lay behind them and the promise of the future that stretched ahead. "It feels like the garden is alive with our memories," she said, her voice a soft echo in the night.

Alex nodded, his gaze lingering on the shimmering water. "Every corner holds a story," he agreed. "It's incredible to think of how far we've come, and how much we've grown."

They continued their walk, the garden a labyrinth of nostalgia and hope. Emma felt the presence of the past, each memory a thread connecting the tapestry of their lives. She remembered the first tentative steps of their journey, the moments of vulnerability and revelation that had shaped their bond.

As they reached the ancient oak, its branches stretching toward the star-studded sky, Emma felt a surge of emotion. This tree, with its timeless strength and beauty, had been a silent witness to their journey—a steadfast guardian of their love.

"Do you remember the first time we sat here together?" Emma asked, her voice tinged with fondness. "It feels like a lifetime ago."

Alex smiled, his eyes reflecting the moonlight. "I do," he replied. "And I remember thinking how lucky I was to have found someone who understood me so deeply."

They settled beneath the oak, the night around them a tapestry of moonlight and memories. Emma felt a profound sense of gratitude for the man beside her, for the love that had weathered the storms and celebrated the joys of their shared journey.

In the quiet of the night, they spoke of dreams and hopes, of the future they would continue to build together. The garden, with its whispers of history and promise of renewal, seemed to hold its breath, listening to the vows spoken beneath the moonlit sky.

As the night deepened and the stars shimmered like distant beacons, Emma and Alex knew that this was a night to remember—a moment captured in time, a testament to the love that had brought them here.

Together, they embraced the magic of the moonlit garden, their hearts entwined with the memories of the past and the possibilities of the future. It was a night that would linger in their hearts, a cherished chapter in the story of their lives, illuminated by the light of love and the glow of the moon.

The Threads of Time

The garden, with its timeless beauty, had become a tapestry of memories for Emma and Alex—a place where the threads of their lives intertwined in intricate patterns. Each moment shared within its bounds added another layer to their story, a rich fabric woven with love, resilience, and growth. Tonight, as they stood beneath the canopy of stars, they felt the weight and wonder of time's passage.

Emma gazed at the familiar landscape, her heart full of the history they had created together. The moon still hung in the sky, a silent observer to their journey, casting its gentle glow over the paths they had walked so many times before. The garden, ever a refuge, seemed to hum with the echoes of their past, a living testament to the life they had built.

"Do you ever think about how each moment is like a thread?" Emma mused, her voice a soft melody in the night air. "Every experience, every choice, weaving together to create the story of our lives."

Alex nodded, his expression thoughtful as he considered her words. "It's amazing to think how each thread, no matter how small, contributes to the whole tapestry," he replied. "And how each one strengthens the fabric of who we are."

Their conversation meandered through the corridors of time, touching on the milestones and memories that had defined their journey. Emma felt a profound sense of gratitude for the tapestry they had woven—a blend of dreams realized and challenges overcome.

As they walked, Emma marveled at the garden's ability to hold their memories, each path a chapter in their shared story. The ancient oak, steadfast and enduring, stood as a symbol of the strength and continuity that had characterized their love.

"Remember when we first planted that rose bush?" Alex asked, his voice filled with nostalgia as they passed by the flourishing blooms. "It felt like a small act at the time, but now it's become a part of the garden's history."

Emma smiled, recalling the day they had knelt together in the soil, their hands dirty and their hearts light with laughter. "It's incredible how something so simple can have such a lasting impact," she reflected. "Just like every moment we've shared."

The garden, with its vibrant colors and whispered secrets, seemed to cradle their memories, preserving them against the relentless march of time. Emma understood that each thread of their lives was precious, contributing to the rich tapestry that was uniquely theirs.

As they paused by the pond, its surface a mirror of the starlit sky, Emma felt a sense of peace and contentment. The threads of time, woven with care and intention, had created a life of depth and meaning—a legacy of love and connection that would endure beyond the present moment.

In the stillness of the night, Emma and Alex embraced the beauty of their shared tapestry, knowing that each new day would add another thread to the intricate pattern of their lives. The garden, ever a witness to their journey, stood as a testament to the enduring power of love and the richness of a life well-lived.

Together, they continued their walk, their hearts full of the stories they had created and the promise of those yet to come. The tapestry of their lives, woven with the threads of time, was a masterpiece of love, resilience, and hope—a testament to the journey they had traveled hand in hand.

An Everlasting Embrace

The garden, a sanctuary of memories and dreams, was alive with the gentle stirrings of dawn. Emma and Alex stood at its heart, surrounded by the vibrant tapestry of their lives—a living testament to the love that had grown and flourished within its bounds. As the first rays of sunlight broke over the horizon, they knew this was a moment to cherish, an everlasting embrace that would echo through the corridors of time.

Emma felt the warmth of the sun on her skin, a reminder of the light that had guided them through the labyrinth of life. Each path they had walked, each challenge they had faced, had led them to this moment—a culmination of their shared journey and the promise of the future that lay ahead.

As they stood beneath the ancient oak, its branches reaching toward the sky like arms enfolding them in a protective embrace, Emma felt a profound sense of peace. The garden, with its whispers of history and hope, seemed to hold its breath, honoring the love that had blossomed within its embrace.

Turning to Alex, Emma found his gaze filled with the warmth and depth that had always drawn her in. "It's amazing how a place can hold so much of our story," she said softly, her voice a gentle echo of the morning breeze. "Every corner of this garden is a part of us."

Alex smiled, his eyes alight with the joy of shared memories. "And every moment here has strengthened our bond," he replied. "It's like the garden has become an extension of our love."

Their words were a quiet acknowledgment of the journey they had traveled—a path marked by resilience, understanding, and unwavering support. Emma knew that their love was not just a fleeting emotion, but a lasting presence that had been nurtured and cherished through the seasons of their lives.

The garden, with its vibrant blooms and timeless beauty, seemed to celebrate their union, each leaf and petal a reflection of the love that had flourished within its bounds. Emma felt a surge of gratitude for the man beside her, for the steadfast companion who had walked with her through the labyrinth of life.

"Thank you for being my partner in this journey," Emma said, her voice filled with heartfelt sincerity. "For every moment we've shared and every dream we've pursued together."

Alex took her hand, his touch a promise of continued companionship and love. "And thank you for being my light," he replied, his words a vow and a celebration of their enduring bond.

In the gentle embrace of the garden, surrounded by the memories and dreams they had cultivated, Emma and Alex felt the strength of their love—an unbreakable bond that would withstand the test of time. It was an everlasting embrace, a testament to the journey they had traveled and the future they would continue to build together.

As the sun rose higher, casting its golden light over the garden, Emma and Alex knew that their story was far from over. Together, they would continue to write the chapters of their lives, each moment a precious thread in the tapestry of their love.

Hand in hand, they walked through the garden, their hearts full of hope and promise. The everlasting embrace of their love, woven with care and intention, would guide them through the days and years to come—a legacy of joy, resilience, and the beauty of a journey shared.

CHAPTER 10: A NEW DAWN

The Promise of Tomorrow

The first light of a new dawn bathed the garden in a soft, golden glow, a fresh beginning painted across the canvas of the sky. Emma and Alex stood together, the warmth of the rising sun enveloping them as they welcomed the promise of tomorrow. The garden, vibrant with life and history, seemed to pulse with anticipation, a testament to the endless possibilities that lay ahead.

Emma felt a sense of renewal, a quiet excitement that bubbled beneath the surface as she considered the path before them. The trials and triumphs of their past had woven a rich tapestry, a foundation upon which they would continue to build their future.

As the sun climbed higher, casting long shadows that danced across the dew-kissed grass, Emma turned to Alex, her heart full of the journey that had brought them to this moment. "Every dawn feels like a new beginning," she mused, her voice a gentle melody in the morning air. "A chance to write new stories, to dream new dreams."

Alex nodded, his gaze sweeping across the garden that had become their sanctuary. "And to embrace the unknown with open hearts," he added. "We've been through so much, yet every day brings something new."

Their conversation flowed with the ease of familiarity, each word a reflection of the love and understanding that had come to define their bond. Emma realized that the promise of tomorrow was not just about the future, but about cherishing the present and honoring the past.

As they walked along the garden's winding paths, Emma marveled at the beauty around them—a beauty that mirrored the richness of their shared journey. The ancient oak, the rose bushes, the pond shimmering with the reflection of the sky, all stood as silent witnesses to their love.

Emma paused by the pond, its surface a tranquil mirror reflecting the endless expanse of the sky. "There's something magical about mornings," she said, her voice filled with wonder. "They remind me that no matter what happens, we have the power to shape our own path."

Alex joined her, his presence a comforting constant. "And with each day, we have the opportunity to grow, to explore, and to deepen our connection," he replied, his words a testament to their shared commitment.

In that moment, Emma felt the promise of tomorrow unfold before her—a landscape of possibilities ripe with potential and discovery. She understood that the journey they had embarked upon was not just about reaching a destination, but about embracing each step along the way.

The garden, alive with the whispers of the past and the promise of the future, seemed to echo their sentiments. Emma knew that as they continued to walk the path of life together, they would face the unknown with courage and grace, guided by the light of their enduring love.

As the morning sun warmed their skin, Emma and Alex embraced the new dawn, their hearts open to the adventures and dreams that awaited them. The promise of tomorrow, woven with hope and intention, was theirs to cherish and explore—a testament to the beauty of life and the power of love.

Together, they stepped forward into the day, hand in hand, ready to write the next chapter of their story. The garden, with its timeless beauty and eternal promise, stood as a symbol of their enduring journey—a journey marked by love, resilience, and the endless promise of tomorrow.

Building a Future Together

The dawn of a new day brought with it a sense of purpose and excitement for Emma and Alex. As they emerged from the garden, their sanctuary of memories and dreams, they carried with them the promise of tomorrow and the resolve to build a future together—a future that would honor the past while embracing the endless possibilities that lay ahead.

Emma felt a surge of determination as they stepped into the world beyond the garden's embrace. The journey they had traveled had been one of growth and discovery, each experience shaping the foundation upon which they would construct their shared future.

The morning air was crisp and invigorating, filling Emma's lungs with a sense of vitality and hope. She turned to Alex, her partner in this grand adventure, her heart full of the dreams they had nurtured and the plans they were ready to set in motion.

"Building a future together feels both exciting and daunting," Emma said, her voice carrying a note of anticipation. "There's so much to consider, so many dreams to weave into reality."

Alex smiled, his eyes reflecting the same enthusiasm that coursed through her veins. "We've come so far, and I know we can create something beautiful together," he replied. "It's about taking each step with intention and love."

Their words were a quiet affirmation of the journey they had embarked upon—a journey that was as much about the present as it was about the future. Emma realized that the foundation of their shared life was built on more than just dreams; it was grounded in the love and understanding that had grown between them.

As they walked hand in hand, Emma felt a sense of clarity about the path ahead. The garden, with its vibrant colors and timeless wisdom, had taught them the value of patience and resilience, lessons they would carry with them as they ventured into the world.

They spoke of the dreams they held dear—the home they envisioned, the projects they wished to pursue, the life they hoped to craft together. Each conversation was a thread in the tapestry of their future, woven with care and intention.

Emma marveled at the sense of unity that had come to define their relationship. It was a bond forged in the fires of experience, tempered by the challenges they had faced and the joys they had celebrated. Together, they were ready to build a future that was as rich and vibrant as the garden they cherished.

"I'm grateful for every moment we've shared," Emma said, her voice filled with sincerity. "And I'm excited for the journey that lies ahead."

Alex squeezed her hand, his touch a promise of unwavering support. "We've got this," he assured her. "Whatever the future holds, we'll face it together."

In that moment, Emma felt a profound sense of peace and certainty. The future, with all its unknowns and possibilities, was theirs to shape and explore. Together, they would continue to build upon the foundation of love and trust they had cultivated, creating a life that was uniquely their own.

As they ventured beyond the garden, their hearts full of hope and promise, Emma and Alex knew that their story was far from over. The world awaited, a canvas upon which they would paint the next chapters of their lives—a testament to the power of love, resilience, and the beauty of building a future together.

The Eternal Dance

The rhythm of life had always been a dance for Emma and Alex—a graceful interplay of steps, sometimes synchronized, sometimes improvised, yet always guided by the music of their hearts. As they moved forward into the future they were building together, they found themselves immersed in this eternal dance, each moment a step in the choreography of their lives.

The garden, with its timeless elegance, had taught them the beauty of harmony and balance. It was a lesson they carried with them into the world beyond, where the dance of life unfolded with every choice and every heartbeat.

One evening, as the sun dipped below the horizon, painting the sky with hues of crimson and gold, Emma and Alex found themselves drawn to the center of their living room, the heart of the home they had begun to create together. The soft glow of candlelight flickered around them, casting gentle shadows that swayed in time with the music that filled the air.

Emma felt a thrill of anticipation as Alex extended his hand, inviting her to join him in the dance. It was a gesture that spoke of trust and unity, a silent vow to navigate the rhythms of life together.

As they moved to the music, Emma marveled at the ease with which they flowed, their steps a seamless conversation of movement and emotion. The dance was a reflection of their journey—a testament to the love that had grown and evolved, guiding them through the labyrinth of life.

The music swelled, and Emma felt herself surrender to the moment, her worries and doubts dissolving in the embrace of the dance. It was a liberation, a reminder that life was not about perfection, but about finding joy and connection in the steps along the way.

Alex's gaze met hers, his eyes filled with the warmth and understanding that had always drawn her in. "Dancing with you feels like coming home," he said softly, his voice a melody that intertwined with the notes of the song.

Emma smiled, her heart full of the journey they had traveled. "And every step is a promise of more to come," she replied, her voice a gentle harmony to his.

The dance carried them through the evening, each step a celebration of their shared dreams and the life they were crafting together. Emma realized that the dance was not just a metaphor, but a living expression of their bond—a testament to the trust and love that had become the foundation of their partnership.

As the music faded, leaving behind a lingering echo of melody, Emma and Alex found themselves standing in the embrace of silence, their hearts full of the promise of tomorrow. The eternal dance, with its twists and turns, was a journey they would continue to explore, guided by the rhythm of their love.

Together, they stepped back into the world, hand in hand, ready to face whatever lay ahead. The eternal dance of life, with its ever-changing tempo, was theirs to navigate—a testament to the enduring power of love and the beauty of a journey shared.

Printed in the USA
CPSIA information can be obtained
at www.ICGtesting.com
LVHW011122021124
795330LV00016B/1093